The
Grumpy Bunny
Goes to School

by Justine Korman • illustrated by Lucinda McQueen

Troll

For Patsy Jensen, an editor who's never grumpy
— J.K.

For Abby Guitar—Lots of love from Aunt Lucy

This edition published in 2001.
Text copyright © 1996 by Justine Korman.
Illustrations copyright © 1996 by Lucinda McQueen.

GRUMPY BUNNY is a trademark of Justine Korman, Lucinda McQueen,
and Troll Communications L.L.C.

Published by WhistleStop, an imprint
and registered trademark of Troll Communications L.L.C.

Printed in the United States of America.

ISBN 0-8167-4121-2

10   9   8   7   6   5   4

Hopper woke up to a perfect September day. Orange and gold leaves twirled in the fresh fall breeze. The sky was a bright, clear blue.

But Hopper felt grumpy. In fact, the grumpy bunny was even grumpier than usual because today was the first day of school.

Once again, Hopper would be helping Mrs. Clover teach the kinderbunny class at Easter Bunny Elementary School. That was where young bunnies went to learn how to be Easter Bunnies.

The new bunnies were always very excited. But to Hopper, school was just the same old ho-hum, humdrum thing.

First the bunnies would gather around the Great Tree while the chief of all the Easter Bunnies, Sir Byron the Great Hare, would lead them in the Easter Bunny's Pledge:

Making treats with care and art,
Bringing love to every heart,
Spreading sunshine every day,
That's the Easter Bunny way!

Then all the eager, scared, happy young bunnies would hop off to their classes. Mrs. Clover always started the day with egg coloring. She taught the same patterns every year: straight lines and flowers, all just so. Then came marshmallow puffing and basket weaving.

The three-carrot snack would be followed by a nap,
then hippety-hop drills, wheelbarrow practice, and, finally,
treat hiding.

Hopper sighed. It was time to go. In fact, the first schoolbunnies were already gathering around the Great Tree as Hopper dragged himself down the path to school. His poor feet felt very tired.

How will I ever get through all those boring hippety-hop drills? he wondered miserably.

Hopper reached the Great Tree just as the schoolbunnies were finishing the pledge. He put his paw over his heart and muttered, "Spreading sunshine, and all that ho-hum, humdrum."

Suddenly Hopper realized Sir Byron was looking right at him!

"I'm sorry I was late," Hopper began.

But Sir Byron said, "No time for that now. You've got a class to teach. Mrs. Clover is sick. You're on your own today."

Hopper's ears flew up in surprise. "What? That's not fair!" he started to complain. Then Hopper had an idea.

"Well, perhaps I could get someone else . . ." Sir Byron began.

But Hopper shook his head. "Never mind, sir. I'll be fine." And he hopped off before the Great Hare could wonder why the grumpy bunny wasn't being grumpy anymore.

Hopper hopped toward the kinderbunny room. *Today I can do things my way!* he thought happily.

And that's just what Hopper did! First he painted the craziest-looking egg anyone had ever seen.

Then Hopper told the kinderbunnies, "Paint your eggs however you want. Just make them as pretty as you can."

The kinderbunnies went far beyond stripes and flowers. They painted designs Hopper had never even imagined. There were star-spangled eggs, rainbow eggs, and eggs with leopard spots. One even grinned like a bright orange jack-o'-lantern.

Hopper didn't hand out patterns for the baskets. Instead, he just gave the kinderbunnies pieces of straw and said, "Weave the baskets however you want. The colors and shapes are up to you. Just make them as beautiful as you can."

When it came time for the marshmallow puffing, Hopper didn't make the usual speech about being careful not to puff too much. He decided to let the kinderbunnies find out for themselves.

PUFF, PUFF, they puffed up their chicks . . .

. . . till one bunny named Peter puffed too much.

PA-WUFFFF! Marshmallow went flying everywhere!

"Let's all do that!" the other bunnies shrieked happily.

"All right," Hopper said. "But see if you can tell exactly when the chick is about to explode. That way you'll learn how much puffing is too much."

A few minutes later, Hopper asked the sticky bunnies to gather together. "You all know how to hippety-hop," he began. "Now try to hoppety-hip. Because once you can hoppety-hip, hippety-hopping is a snap."

"It's hard," a kinderbunny named Daisy said.
"No, it's fun!" cried her friend Flopsy.

When the bunnies were tired of hoppety-hipping, Hopper said, "Every Easter Bunny must learn to push a wheelbarrow filled with treats. We could march our wheelbarrows back and forth across the room—or we could have a race!"

The kinderbunnies cheered. Soon they were racing around the room, laughing with glee.

Just then Sir Byron appeared. "What's all this noise?" shouted the Great Hare.

Every bunny fell silent. Hopper's ears dropped and his stomach flippety-flopped. "Um, I . . ." the nervous bunny stammered.

"We were having a wheelbarrow race!" shouted Flopsy.

One look at Sir Byron's angry face and Hopper knew he was in deep trouble. He looked down at his sore feet and wished he'd never gotten out of bed.

Sir Byron looked around the marshmallow-strewn room. "What's all this mess?" he asked.

Hopper didn't know what to say. "I . . . we . . ."

"We made our chicks so puffy they exploded!" Peter cried. "*PA-WUFFFF!*" he added, puffing up his furry cheeks.

Hopper groaned. This day was getting worse by the minute.

Then Sir Byron spotted the eggs drying on the windowsill. "And what happened here? Did you forget to show them the proper painting patterns?"

Daisy said, "Hopper let us paint whatever we wanted. It was fun!"

"I see," said the Great Hare. Then he stared at the eggs. "Some of these are actually quite pretty."

Hopper's ears lifted. Had he heard Sir Byron right?

"Tradition is good. But there's always room for new ideas," the Great Hare declared. "A wheelbarrow race might help improve their skills—and the bunnies certainly seemed to enjoy it. And perhaps letting the bunnies explode a few marshmallows is the best way to teach them when to stop puffing," the Great Hare added.

Hopper's jaw dropped. Sir Byron clapped him on the back. "You'll make a fine teacher someday, Hopper. In the future, though, I hope you'll bring your ideas to me first."

Hopper nodded eagerly. He still couldn't quite believe that he wasn't in trouble.

"Of course, you'll have to clean up this mess," the Great Hare said.

Hopper's heart sank. It would take him all afternoon to clean up the sticky room.

Then Daisy said, "We'll help you, Hopper."
"Yes!" Flopsy cried. "You're our favorite teacher!"
"Even cleaning up will be fun with you!" Peter declared.
And, to Hopper's amazement, it was.

Hopper hippety-hopped all the way home. He was so happy that even his sore feet felt good!

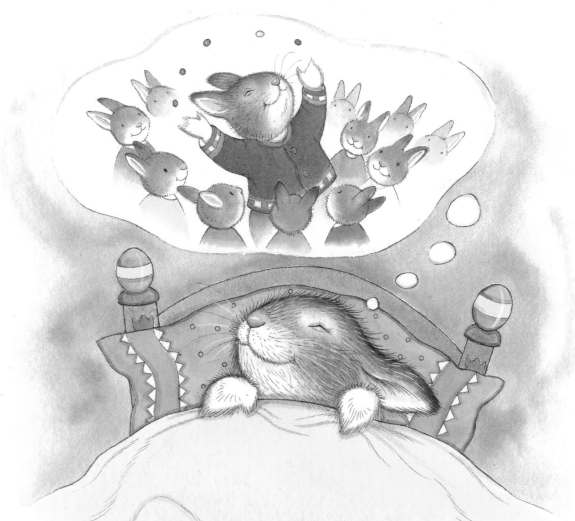

Back in his burrow, Hopper decided, "Tomorrow I'll ask Sir Byron if I can teach jellybean juggling."

He couldn't wait to go back to school the next day. In fact, from that day on, Hopper was never grumpy about going to school again.